for Josh and Imogen, who loves everything on four legs
FM

for my friend Gordon, and everyone who celebrates the little things in life
DA

Designed by Frances McKay
Printed and bound in Belgium by Proost
for the publishers Piccadilly Press Ltd.,
5 Castle Road, London NW1 8PR

ISBN: 1 85340 662 7 (hardback)
1 85340 657 0 (paperback)

1 3 5 7 9 10 8 6 4 2

Set in 21 pt Trebuchet MS

A catalogue record for this book is available from the
British Library

Dawn Apperley lives in London. After completing her degree in graphic design
she started work as a designer and illustrator. She has since illustrated a number of
picture books. This is her first book for Piccadilly.

Frances McKay lives in London. Originally trained as a graphic designer, she has worked as a
picture book designer and art director for many years. She has also written
a number of stories for children. This is her first book for Piccadilly.

Kira the Koala

Frances McKay
Illustrated by Dawn Apperley

Piccadilly Press • London

Kira the koala lived high in the branches of an old eucalyptus tree.

"Leaves, leaves, leaves," thought Kira. "I'm tired of eating leaves!"

So Kira went walkabout to look for
something else to eat. Soon she found
some parrots eating bright red fruit.
Kira tried some.

"Ugh!" Kira spluttered. The fruit was sour!

"Koalas don't like fruit!" squawked
the parrots. "Everybody knows that."

Next, Kira found a mob of kangaroos,
munching long green grass.

"I'll try some of that," thought Kira.
But the grass made Kira sneeze.
"Atchoo!" sniffled Kira.

The kangaroos just laughed and bounced away.

"Koalas don't like grass!" they said.
"Everybody knows that."

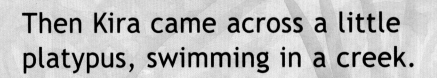

Then Kira came across a little platypus, swimming in a creek.

"Do *you* have anything I could eat?" asked Kira.

"The wet squiggly things
in the water are delicious,"
replied the platypus.

But when Kira tried catching
some she almost fell in!

"Too bad," said the platypus
as she swam away.
"But koalas don't like wet
squiggly things, anyway.
Everybody knows that."

Kira jumped up and down
to dry her fur in the sun.
She nearly bumped into
some big yellow flowers.

A honey-possum popped up
from behind one of them.
"Watch out!" he said.
"I'm eating the nectar!"

"Nectar?" said Kira.
"May I try some of that?"

But when she tried some
a bee stung her nose!

"Oh dear," said the honey-possum.
"But koalas really don't like
eating nectar. Everybody knows that."

Kira sat down at the bottom of a tree.
"I'm so hungry!" she wailed.
"There must be something to eat
that's not fruit or grass or wet and squiggly
and that doesn't sting! But what?"

Looking up, Kira saw
something at the top
of the tree. She
climbed up quickly.

"Leaves, yummy leaves," said Kira
and she started to eat them.
They were delicious.

The noisy parrots
gathered around her.
"Koalas *only* eat
eucalyptus leaves!"
they said.

"Oh, yes!" cried Kira happily.
"*I* know that!"